SHARON PHILLIPS DENSLOW

Georgie Lee

Pictures by
LYNNE RAE PERKINS

Greenwillow Books
An Imprint of HarperCollins*Publishers*

Georgie Lee
Text copyright © 2002 by Sharon Phillips Denslow
Illustrations copyright © 2002 by Lynne Rae Perkins
All rights reserved. No part of this book may be used or reproduced in any manner whatsoever
without written permission except in the case of brief quotations embodied in critical articles
and reviews. Printed in the United States of America. For information address HarperCollins
Children's Books, a division of HarperCollins Publishers.
www.harperchildrens.com

The text of this book is set in Goudy Old Style.

Library of Congress Cataloging-in-Publication Data

Denslow, Sharon Phillips.
Georgie Lee / by Sharon Phillips Denslow;
illustrated by Lynne Rae Perkins.
    p.   cm.
"Greenwillow Books."
Summary: A young boy and his grandmother share
all sorts of adventures on her farm with her
cat, Boots, and her cow, Georgie Lee.
ISBN 0-688-17940-1 (trade).   ISBN 0-688-17941-X (lib. bdg.)
[1. Farm life—Fiction. 2. Grandmothers—Fiction.]
I. Perkins, Lynne Rae, ill. II. Title.
PZ7.D433 Ge 2002 [Fic]—dc21 00-052797

1 2 3 4 5 6 7 8 9 10 First Edition

To Daddy, who told me the story about the cow and
the creek fish; to Grandmother, who taught me not
to be afraid of wasps and snakes and nighttime;
and to the real Boots, who followed us everywhere
on our beloved farm on Jackson School Road
— S. P. D.

For my dear ones
— L. R. P.

Contents

1. THE SMART COW 13

2. UP A TREE 23

3. EARLY 34

4. THE BIG STORM 47

5. THE HAUNTED HOUSE 61

6. STARS AND DOGS 80

Georgie
Lee

"Why do tumblebugs make balls out of cow manure?" J.D. asked.
"Ever try rolling something that's not round?" Grandmother said.

1. THE SMART COW

One hot summer afternoon, as they were walking from the truck down the hill to the creek to cool off, J.D. said to his grandmother, "Why can't Georgie Lee be more like Boots?"

Grandmother considered for a minute.

"How can a cow be like a cat?" she asked.

"She could be smaller," J.D. said.

"Georgie Lee is small for a cow," Grandmother said.

"Not small enough," J.D. said, looking behind him as Georgie Lee cheerfully plodded along the path following them.

J.D. moved closer to Grandmother. "She could be gentle like Boots."

"Never had a more gentle cow," Grandmother said.

"What about last summer when she stepped on your foot?" J.D. said.

"She didn't know it was my foot," Grandmother said.

"Then Georgie Lee should be as smart as Boots. Boots would know your foot."

Grandmother laughed. "That's true."

Boots, hearing her name again, stopped in the path and waited for them to catch up. Her long tail curled in the air like a question mark, as if she were asking them what was taking them so long.

A big fly bit J.D. on the leg, and he smacked at it.

Georgie Lee, who had lots of flies biting her, took

J.D.'s fly smacking as a sign to get the move on. She shook her head and took off running toward the creek, her fat sides swinging wildly from side to side with a *yuh, yuh, yuh* sound.

"At least you don't have to worry about Boots trampling you down," J.D. said.

"You've never been between Boots and a tree when she took a running fit," Grandmother said.

🌿

When J.D. and Grandmother reached the bank of the creek, they saw Georgie Lee standing quietly in a cool spring-fed pool.

"What's she doing? Why doesn't she take a drink? What's wrong with her?" J.D. asked.

"Your guess is as good as mine. No idea. Probably nothing," Grandmother said, answering J.D.'s three questions.

"What a dumb cow, just standing there in the creek," J.D. said.

"I thought that was what we were planning on doing," Grandmother said.

"Not me. I was going to splash and duck under and catch fish with my bare hands."

Georgie Lee ignored them. She stood in the water without moving. Then she crooked her tail up and flicked it, sending drops of water onto J.D.'s face and a trail of water across her back, making any flies there crawl to her belly.

"Why's she standing there letting the flies bite her? Maybe she's had a heatstroke," J.D. said.

"Standing in the cool creek doesn't generally give you heatstroke," Grandmother said.

J.D. got restless. He started scratching peeling skin off his knees and burrowing his toes in the creek gravel.

"Did I ever tell you where I got Georgie Lee's name?" Grandmother asked.

J.D. nodded. "You named her after a friend of your mother's."

"Yes, but did I ever tell you why?"

"Because they looked alike?" J.D. guessed.

"Not exactly," Grandmother said. "The first Georgie Lee loved onions. She was always cooking with them. Her house, her clothes, and sometimes even her skin smelled like onions. When I got my new little cow, I went to check on her one day, and she was eating wild onion greens. Her breath smelled so sweet with onions and it put me in mind so much of Mama's friend that Georgie Lee had her name."

All through Grandmother's naming story Georgie Lee stood in the creek, not moving.

"Let's make her get out so we can get in the water," J.D. said.

"Shh," Grandmother said, "look."

The sandy mud Georgie Lee had stirred up when she walked into the creek was clearing. The tiny fish that lived in the creek appeared and began swimming around the cow.

"Maybe they're going to bite her tail," J.D. said.

"I doubt it," Grandmother said.

The fish swam past Georgie Lee's tail and schooled under her spotted belly.

"They better watch out. Georgie Lee will step on them, too."

But Georgie Lee still didn't move.

The little fish were all around Georgie Lee.

"They never swim around me like that," J.D. said.

Even with flies all over her belly and little fish in the water under her belly, the only motion Georgie Lee made was that of her sides moving slowly in and out with her breathing.

The little fish started to move, though. In a small, quick flash one of the fish jumped out of the water and snatched a fly from Georgie Lee's belly.

"Oh!" J.D. and Grandmother gasped together.

As soon as the first fish was back in the water, another fish jumped up and caught a fly. Then one after another, over and over, the little fish leaped into the air and ate Georgie Lee's flies.

J.D. and Grandmother sat as quiet and still watching those fish as Georgie Lee had waiting for them.

When the flies were gone, the full fish swam back to their hiding place under the soapstone ledge. Then Georgie Lee lowered her head for a long, long drink of cool water.

As she passed J.D. and Grandmother on her way back to her hill of grass, Georgie Lee turned her head toward J.D.

"Did you see that, Grandmother? Georgie Lee smiled at me."

"Cows don't smile, J.D."

"Smart ones do," J.D. said.

For the rest of the afternoon J.D. splashed in the cool water, and he and Grandmother waded along the shallow creek bed, looking for crawdaddies under rocks. Boots chased blue butterflies over the sand and gravel.

When it was time to go back to the house, they found Georgie Lee at the top of the hill, eating grass.

J.D. pulled two ears of sweet corn from the back of the truck and handed them to Grandmother.

"You feed her today," Grandmother said.

J.D. squeezed between the gate and the gatepost and walked slowly toward Georgie Lee. Georgie Lee spotted the corn. She shook her head and ran for J.D., her sides swinging, making her *yuh, yuh, yuh* sound. J.D. took a step back toward the gate. Then he thought of the little, timid fish and Georgie Lee standing quietly for them.

Georgie Lee stopped in a whirl of dust in front of J.D. She snuffled the corn. Then her long tongue wrapped around an ear, and she rolled it into her mouth and began to chew.

"Hello, old onion breath," J.D. said.

Gently he reached out to scratch Georgie Lee's head as he'd seen Grandmother do. The fine, curly hairs on her forehead were as soft and silky as the fur on Boots's chest.

Riding home in the truck with Boots on the seat between them, J.D. asked, "How come everything on your farm is so smart, Grandmother?"

"Don't rightly know," Grandmother said. "But I suspect it's something in the water."

2. UP A TREE

It was too hot in the house, so J.D. and
Grandmother ate lunch on the front porch.
Grandmother sat in the swing, gently pushing it
back and forth with her foot. J.D. sat on the cool
concrete steps.

When J.D. finished his last biscuit-and-ham
sandwich, he decided to hop up and down the

steps. Each time he jumped off the bottom step, he reached out, grabbed a spirea branch, and stripped the feathery leaves off with his thumb.

He had a handful of tiny leaves by the time Grandmother said, "J.D., if you keep on doing that, my bush is going to look like a porcupine."

J.D. sprinkled the wilting leaves back on top of the bush. He walked out into the yard and stood under the big catalpa tree.

"I think I'll climb that tree," he said.

"Good idea," said Grandmother.

J.D. jumped for the lowest branch of the old tree. He pulled himself up and began to climb. The leaves thinned out a little higher up, and he could see all around. The peak of the roof was to his right, but in every other direction he could see flat woods, wide fields, and two roads spooling away.

Bits of gray bark fell on J.D.'s head. Boots turned in her claw sharpening to meow in his face and then went on with her business.

"How did Boots get up here before me?" J.D. called.

"She went up the back side of the tree at a run," Grandmother called back.

Boots yawned and twitched her tail at J.D. Then she climbed to a higher branch. J.D. followed.

The swing creaked. Grandmother stood under the tree to see how high J.D. was.

"I used to climb trees," Grandmother said.

"When you and Early were little?" J.D. asked.

Early was Grandmother's older brother.

"I was better at it than Early," Grandmother said.

Grandmother dragged a chair from the porch and set it under the tree.

"I climbed a tree on my sixth birthday and almost spent the night in it. Daddy was running the ferry upriver and he was late and I was mad. I told them I wasn't coming down out of that tree until Daddy came home."

Grandmother stood on the chair and reached for a tree limb.

"It got dark, and I was still in the tree. The mosquitoes started biting. Mama was threatening to give my cake to the dogs if I didn't come down.

Lucky for me, Daddy's boat came around the bend right after she said that."

Grandmother pulled herself into the tree and climbed until she was sitting beside J.D.

"Was your daddy mad at you?" J.D. asked.

Grandmother grinned at J.D. "He stood under the tree and said, 'I always did like to climb trees when I was a boy,' and then he climbed up, and we sat in that tree until Mama brought out my cake covered in candles and glowing in the dark like a lantern."

J.D. and Grandmother sat side by side in the tree, swinging their legs and admiring the view.

After a bit Grandmother said, "I'd wager not too many grandmothers are sitting in catalpa trees with their grandsons this afternoon."

Boots meowed at not being included.

"There are lots of cats up trees right now," Grandmother said.

A mockingbird called from the orchard, and a tractor started up in the distance. The big velvety catalpa leaves rustled together softly as a small breeze passed.

"It's like being in a boat, riding the air up here," Grandmother said.

"Only we're not going anywhere," said J.D.

"We may not be, but they sure are," Grandmother said, pointing.

Eight of Grandmother's friend Ronald's cows and his big bull, Russell, were strolling along beside the road as if they were heading for town to have a look around.

Grandmother's cow, Georgie Lee, saw the other cows, too. She bawled and snuffled and ran along the fence with her tail bent in the air.

"A stampede!" shouted J.D.

"Not much of one," Grandmother said, "but let's climb down and see what we can do about rounding them up."

"Want me to run and get in front of them?" J.D. asked, starting down.

"If you were an escaped cow and you heard a boy running up behind you, what would you do?" Grandmother said.

"Oh," J.D. said.

"We'll walk as fast and quiet as we can and hope to head them off," Grandmother said.

J.D. scraped his chin and one elbow on the tree trunk as he swung to the ground. Bits of bark stuck to his damp skin. He thought Grandmother was behind him, but she was still sitting on her branch.

"Hurry, Grandmother," J.D. said.

Grandmother had a smile J.D. had never seen on her face. "It seems, J.D., I remembered how to climb up a tree, but I forgot how to get down," Grandmother said.

"But you have to come down. We have to get the cows," J.D. said.

"You'll have to do it alone," Grandmother said. "And you'll have to hurry. Look!"

The Rileys' old shaggy dog, Muffler, who chased everything that passed her yard, had flung herself across the road toward the cows. In one swift movement Russell turned the cows around, and they thundered back toward J.D. and Grandmother.

"Now that's a stampede!" Grandmother yelled. "Run and open the gate. Maybe they'll go back in."

J.D. ran as fast as he could. His cheeks felt on fire with heat and sweat. He reached the big metal gate, flipped the latch, and swung it wide. The cows, with Russell in the lead, tossing his head like a buffalo, were roaring right for him. J.D. waved his arms to try to get them to turn into the opening.

"They're not going to go in!" J.D. shouted.

He was ready to jump on the gate to save himself when something ran up beside him and bellowed. It was Georgie Lee. She bellowed again and thundered through the gate past J.D. The herd turned and followed through the gate behind her. J.D. slammed the gate shut.

"Good job," Grandmother said when J.D. got back to the tree.

"What about Georgie Lee?" J.D. said.

"We'll bring her home later and fix the fence post she knocked down to get out," Grandmother said. "Right now you need to go to the smokehouse and get the ladder."

There were big red wasps in the smokehouse.

"Maybe I should get somebody to help," J.D. said.

"Oh, no, you don't. We're the only ones who are going to know that I got stuck up a tree," Grandmother said.

When J.D. reached the smokehouse, three wasps were flying around the crack above the door.

"Move slowly," Grandmother called, "and they won't bother you."

J.D. carefully opened the door. It dragged on the ground, and he had to give it a jerk. Wasps flew around his head. J.D. ducked down and grabbed the ladder. He pulled it to the tree and after three attempts managed to prop it against the trunk.

Boots ran down the ladder headfirst. Grandmother took a little time. She turned herself around and gently felt for each rung with her foot.

"I think we need some cold lemonade," Grandmother said when she was on the ground again.

They sat on the porch, drinking from dripping glasses. Grandmother sat in the swing. J.D. sat on the steps.

"I was thinking about Ronald's cows while you were getting the ladder," Grandmother said. "I was wondering how they got out. They didn't knock their fence over. Or jump it. Did you notice anything about them?"

"They were in a hurry," J.D. said, "and they smelled bad."

"Like something spoiled and mucky?" Grandmother asked.

J.D. nodded.

"That was the mud," Grandmother said, "mud from the bottom of the pond. Pond mud stinks like it looks: slimy and oozy. Those cows were covered in mud because they swam out under the fence. The pond was so low it made it easy."

"They swam out?" J.D. said. "That's pretty smart."

"A lot smarter than somebody climbing a tree she can't get down," Grandmother said.

J.D. laughed. He thought about cows for a minute.

"Did you ever see a cow up a tree?" he asked finally.

"Not yet," Grandmother said, "but the way things are going, I expect to any day."

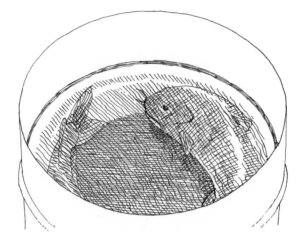

3. EARLY

J.D. and Grandmother had been waiting all day for Grandmother's brother, Early, to come.

"Maybe he stopped to fish somewhere," J.D. said.

Early loved to fish. Every summer he came home to take Grandmother and J.D. fishing on the lake. They used catalpa worms from Grandmother's catalpa tree for bait.

J.D. had two big jars of the black-and-yellow

worms ready. Grandmother had Early's room in the attic ready.

"Do you think Early will figure out our mystery and our riddle?" J.D. asked.

"I think we'll stump him this time," Grandmother said.

Two things Early liked almost as much as fishing were riddles and mysteries. Early collected riddles from everybody he met on his travels. His mysteries were the kind that you don't pay any attention to until one day you look close and there it is.

A car horn sounded far off down the road.

"Is that Early?" J.D. asked.

Grandmother stopped putting the ears of corn into the pan and listened.

"It's Morse code," Grandmother said. "So it's got to be Early. Nobody else would use a car horn to tap out Morse code."

"What's he saying?" J.D. asked.

"SOS," Grandmother said.

"What's that mean?" J.D. said.

"Save Our Ship or something like that," said

Grandmother. "But I don't think his camper is sinking into the road."

"Maybe it's on fire!" J.D. shouted. He ran to the driveway for a better look.

The honking grew louder, and in the distance J.D. saw Early's old green-and-white camper.

"It's him! It's him!" J.D. shouted.

Grandmother and J.D. watched the camper get closer and closer. Early gave up his signal and just honked over and over.

"Maybe his camper is full of bees," J.D. said.

"I suspect Early's just full of beans, is all," Grandmother said.

Grandmother and J.D. waved as Early pulled into the driveway. But Early didn't wave back. He didn't slow down. He drove right past them, through Grandmother's front yard, under the catalpa tree, and into the backyard to the pasture gate.

"Forever more," said Grandmother, rolling her eyes. She and J.D. ran after the camper.

Early stuck his head out the window and waved them over. "We've got to save Melville," he shouted. "Open the gate."

J.D. slipped the latch and pulled the gate open.

Early rumbled through and stopped in a swirl of dust. "Get in, we're going to the pond," he said.

He slammed the camper into gear, wriggled his ears at J.D., and yelled to Grandmother, "Hang on!"

Startled by the commotion, Georgie Lee came running from the cool shade of the woods to see what was going on. When she saw the camper hurtling along, she ran after it, bawling and shaking her head, trying to butt a fender.

J.D. thought Early was going to drive into the pond, but he stopped by the cedar tree and hopped into the back of the camper. He flung back a piece

of canvas draped over a cut-off steel barrel with just enough water in it to cover the biggest catfish J.D. had ever seen.

"Meet Melville," Early said.

"Give me strength," Grandmother said. "All this hoopla over a fish."

"Not just any fish," Early said. "This is a mystery fish if there ever was one."

"Did you catch him?" J.D. asked.

"Nope," Early said. "I stopped to get an ice-cream bar at a bait shop on the other side of the lake, and there he was in a fish tank. Couldn't even move, the tank was so small. The man who owned the place said he was only twelve inches long two years ago when he put him in the tank. Fish in small tanks are supposed to stay small, not keep growing and growing like Melville."

Early dragged the oil barrel toward the camper door. "I couldn't just leave him there, you know," Early said.

Melville flapped his tail, splashing dirty water on J.D.

"Hurry, he's running out of air," Early said.

Grandmother and J.D. helped Early pull the barrel closer to the door. Melville was almost as long as J.D. He made grumbling sounds and flopped as Early staggered to the water. Carefully Early laid the big fish in the muddy shallows.

Melville didn't move.

Early splashed the water around him. Then Melville twisted his tail left and right, and with a great swoosh and surge he disappeared into the deep water.

"He'll probably grow as long as Georgie Lee in this pond," Grandmother said.

Early drove more slowly on the way back to the house.

Boots was sitting on the post by the open gate.

"Uh-oh," said J.D. "We left the gate open."

Grandmother looked all around the field. "Where'd that cow get to now?"

Georgie Lee wasn't in the backyard or the front yard.

"She'll turn up," Early said. He gave

Grandmother and J.D. big hugs. "It sure is good to be home," he said.

"I've got catalpa worms," J.D. said.

"Then we've got a fishing trip tomorrow," Early said.

Grandmother raised her eyebrows. "What are we going to fish in?"

"*The Belle of Birmingham*," J.D. said.

Grandmother pointed to the back of the camper. Where Early's fishing boat should have been, there was only an empty trailer hitch.

"They don't just give away big catfish," Early said.

"You traded the *Belle* for a catfish?" J.D. said.

"I did," Early said. "But don't worry, J.D. The *Belle* is docked by the bait store, and we can use it all we want this week. Besides, I've had my eye on a bigger boat for some time anyway."

"As long as I've known you," Grandmother said, "and I still don't understand you. You're the original mystery."

"Speaking of mysteries," Early said. "I've brought you one."

He took a small matchbox out of his frayed shirt pocket.

"I've got one, too," J.D. said, pulling a wad of paper towel from his pocket.

"You go first," Early said.

J.D. unwrapped the paper towel. A small twig lay inside. Attached to the twig was a tiny barrel, small at the top and bottom and circled with rings.

"Did you carve this?" Early asked.

"Nope," J.D. said. "Something made it."

Early took out his magnifying glass and looked closely. "It looks just like a beer keg," he said, puzzled.

"It's a stinkbug egg," J.D. said, grinning.

"An old stinkbug made something as perfect as this," Early said, marveling.

J.D. nodded at Early's matchbox. "What'd you bring?"

"Nothing like this," Early said, still admiring the stinkbug's work.

He gave the egg sac back to J.D. and gently opened the box.

"I was in this field in Montana. The sky was clear and bluer than I'd ever seen. Suddenly, out of that clear sky, sparkling little flakes like these started falling all around me." Early shook some of the shining flakes into Grandmother's and J.D.'s hands. They glittered in the sun.

"As near as I can figure, they're flakes of mica from some volcanic ash. They swirled around the world miles up in the sky and finally fell right where I was standing in that field," Early said.

J.D. and Grandmother gently brushed the mystery flakes back into the box.

"I've got a riddle for you," J.D. said.

"Shoot," Early said.

J.D. said, "I don't have it. I don't want it. But if I had it, I wouldn't trade it for a million dollars."

"The answer wouldn't be a sixty-pound catfish, would it?" Early said.

"Nope," J.D. said.

"I don't have it. I don't want it. But if I had it, I wouldn't trade it for a million dollars," Early repeated.

"No," J.D. said. "I don't have it. I don't want it."

"That's what I said," Early said.

"No, you said you didn't have it," J.D. said.

"You mean, I have it?" Early asked, surprised.

J.D. and Grandmother grinned.

"That's a tough one," Early said. "I might have to go figure that out on a full stomach."

"Supper'll be ready as soon as I put on the corn," Grandmother said.

They walked to the back door with Early muttering the riddle. The back door was wide open.

"The house'll be full of flies," Early said.

"That's not all it's full of," Grandmother said with her hands on her hips.

Georgie Lee was standing in the back porch helping herself to the ears of corn in the pan.

"How'd she get up the back steps?" J.D. said.

"A cow with corn on her mind can do anything," Grandmother said, shooing Georgie Lee out with a broom.

When Georgie Lee got to the door and the steps, she scrunched her legs together and jumped over the steps to the ground as if she did it every day.

J.D., Grandmother, and Early sat down at the supper table. There were ham and tomatoes and biscuits and fried potatoes and butter beans and pickles and coconut pie, but there was no bowl of fresh corn.

"Plenty more corn in the garden for tomorrow," Grandmother said.

Early nodded. "Plenty more fish in the sea."

J.D. smiled. "But only one answer to my riddle."

Early wriggled his ears at J.D.

"Have you got it, Elda?" Early asked Grandmother.

"Certainly not," Grandmother said.

"Does Georgie Lee have it?" Early asked.

"Not unless eating a bait of fresh corn affects her strangely overnight," Grandmother said.

"Don't tell me the answer yet," Early said, popping a forkful of potatoes in his mouth.

Grandmother and J.D. looked at each other with satisfaction. Then they both looked at Early's shining bald head and laughed.

"You don't mean . . ." Early said, touching the top of his head.

Grandmother and J.D. laughed harder.

"I've got it," Early said slowly. "I don't want it." He started to laugh with Grandmother and J.D.

"But I wouldn't trade my own bald head for a million dollars, that's for sure!"

"I told you Georgie Lee didn't have it," J.D. said.

"Well, I know something Georgie Lee has that none of us has," Early said.

"What?" J.D. said.

"A stomach full of fresh sweet corn!" Early said.

4. THE BIG STORM

A big storm was coming, so J.D. and Grandmother hurried to pick the last of the strawberries before it hit.

"Have you ever seen hailstones as big as golf balls?" J.D. asked as he ate a berry.

"I've never even seen hailstones as big as this

strawberry," Grandmother said. "Who told you to expect golf ball–size hail?"

"Effie," J.D. said.

Effie was Grandmother's neighbor across the cornfield. She had a regular radio, a weather radio, a CB scanner, and a satellite dish. If there was a ripple on the wind, Effie knew about it.

"What else did Effie say?" Grandmother asked.

"That we'd better make tracks to get Georgie Lee, or the storm would catch us for sure."

Grandmother looked at the dark clouds in the west. "We've got all the berries we can manage anyway," she said, standing up.

J.D. ran to the smokehouse to get Georgie Lee's halter. He opened the door an inch at a time so the wasps wouldn't be disturbed.

The shortest path to the bottoms and Georgie Lee went through Taz's cornfield. Excited grasshoppers leaped wildly from the cornstalks, bouncing off J.D.'s legs and arms.

"I'm glad grasshoppers aren't as big as pigs," J.D. said.

"That makes two of us," Grandmother said, swiping a junior grasshopper off her chin.

When they reached Effie's place, they moved quietly to make sure there was no sign of Stonewall, Effie's billy goat.

"She said she'd tie him up," J.D. said.

"Always best to double-check as far as that goat's concerned," Grandmother said.

It was quiet in Effie's yard, with only a hen pecking by the back steps. J.D. kept his eyes peeled for any sign of Stonewall. Halfway up the path they heard an angry baaing from behind the old barn.

Effie heard it, too. She stuck her head out the back door and said, "CNN just reported we might be in for some big wind as well as hail in the storm. I'd hurry if I were you."

"Here's some late berries for you, Effie," Grandmother called.

J.D. ran the berry box to her porch.

"Thank you, J.D.," Effie said. "I do love nothing better than fresh berries."

Effie waved them up the path before disappearing back inside to check the weather.

"I know something she likes better than berries," Grandmother grumbled.

"Goats?" J.D. said.

Grandmother shook her head.

J.D. knew that Effie helped herself to Taz's corn when she wanted some. "Corn. She likes corn better than berries," he guessed.

Grandmother glanced over her shoulder at the gathering clouds in the west. "There's nothing Effie Houser loves more than a good storm," she said.

"How can she love storms?" he asked. Storms worried J.D.

"They keep her on her toes and give her lots of chances to talk to everyone and dish out advice," Grandmother answered.

"She does keep us updated," J.D. said.

"Every hour on the hour," Grandmother said. "Our own private weatherwoman."

It was quiet at first when they reached the gravel road that led to the creek bottoms. Then the wind began to stir the trees.

"Maybe Effie's right. Maybe we better hurry," J.D. said.

"Plenty of time," said Grandmother.

Usually Georgie Lee heard them coming and met them at the gate. But today there was no sign of her.

"That cow is never where you want her to be," Grandmother said. "Suu-cow. Suu-cow."

Georgie Lee mooed, but J.D. and Grandmother couldn't see her.

Grandmother called again, "Suu-cow. Suu-cow."

Georgie Lee mooed again.

"There she is," J.D. said, spying Georgie Lee's spoon-shaped ears above the waving grass.

Realizing she'd been found, Georgie Lee lifted

her hindquarters first and then heaved up her head and shoulders.

"There's a storm coming, Georgie Lee," J.D. said as Grandmother snapped the lead rope onto Georgie Lee's halter.

Unconcerned, Georgie Lee cleaned her nose out with two swipes of her long, grass-stained tongue.

J.D. tugged Grandmother's hand. "Make her come on, Grandmother."

"Let's go, Georgie Lee," Grandmother said. "Effie tells us a big one's coming."

Georgie Lee clomped slowly up the hill. Dark clouds covered half of the sky, and they were moving fast. Swirling wind picked up dust and grass in the field beside the road.

"Look at that," Grandmother said.

A small, speckled screech owl was suspended above the road as if it were on a wire. When it moved its wings, nothing happened because the wind kept it hovering in the same place.

"He's trying to make it to the barn," Grandmother said.

The wind dropped for a second, and the owl swooped away quickly to the safety of the deserted barn just before a stronger gust of wind hit.

J.D. felt as if his clothes were glued down when the wind flattened them against his skin. Grandmother's hair stuck straight out, and Georgie Lee's skinny tail blew sideways, its fat tuft of hair on the end acting like a kite.

"Make Georgie Lee go faster," J.D. shouted.

Grandmother tugged on Georgie Lee's rope. Georgie Lee walked faster for a few steps; then she resumed her clomping plod.

Grandmother and J.D. crowded beside her,

letting her wide body block the wind. Clouds covered the sky, and the bursts of wind felt cooler.

They'd just started down the path to Effie's when Stonewall rushed toward them from behind a bush.

"Look out!" Grandmother shouted.

J.D. scrooched even closer to Georgie Lee. Georgie Lee clomped along, ignoring Stonewall. Stonewall shook his horns and stepped in front of Georgie Lee. Grandmother tried to pull Georgie Lee around the goat.

They had circled safely around when Effie yelled from her porch, "I had to let him loose, couldn't keep him tied up in a storm. You better stay here. You won't make it home. Sixty-mile-an-hour winds heading this way from Graves County!"

Effie said something else, but the wind erased her words from the air.

Grandmother waved at Effie and kept pulling Georgie Lee away from Stonewall. The goat ran up the path and stood in front of them, shaking his horns.

"I wish the wind would pick him up and take him

away," Grandmother shouted.

Georgie Lee stopped and stared at the goat. He had her attention at last. She crooked her tail in the air, bellowed once, and rushed for Stonewall, pulling the rope out of Grandmother's hand. Stonewall was so startled that he ran backward, baaing and bleating like a baby goat that'd seen worse than a troll.

"Whoa, Georgie Lee," Grandmother shouted.

But Georgie Lee was excited now. She kept on running, ignoring the corn beside the path, snorting when a fat cold raindrop hit her on the nose. J.D. and Grandmother ran after her, but they couldn't catch her.

"Whew," said Grandmother, slowing down. "I can't run anymore. Let her go. She knows where home is."

Thunder growled in the west. J.D. looked at the thick sky and grabbed Grandmother's hand. "Grandmother, we need to walk really, really fast," he said.

J.D. and Grandmother ran for a bit, walked for a

bit, and barely beat the storm back to the house. When they got there, Georgie Lee was standing by the gate to her pasture, chewing a stalk of corn she'd managed to snag from the field on the run. Grandmother opened the gate and slid Georgie Lee's halter off, and Georgie Lee walked slowly through.

"I'll pull the truck into the shed, J.D. You run into the house and close the windows. Don't slam them shut so hard you break the glass," Grandmother said.

Just as J.D. reached the last window, it started to rain. He couldn't get the big porch window down. The rain slammed across the porch, spraying water into the house. The swing thumped against the wall.

"I can't get it down," he yelled to Grandmother as she rushed in. She tugged on one side and J.D. tugged on the other until the old window inched closed.

"We've got to get the swing or the wind'll blow it into the window," Grandmother shouted.

J.D. held the swing as steady as he could while Grandmother stood on a chair and lifted the swing chains one loop at a time until the swing was high and safe, near the hooks in the ceiling.

The porch was covered with water and leaves, and J.D.'s shoes squished and slid. "I don't see any hail yet," he said as he peered out at the storm.

"Plenty of rain and wind," Grandmother said. A small branch thunked to the ground in the front yard.

"Is the barn door open for Georgie Lee?" J.D. asked.

"Yes, if she's got enough sense to get inside."

"But she's a smart cow," J.D. said.

"Smart and good sense are two different things," Grandmother said.

They went to the back porch to check on Georgie Lee. Boots, who'd been sleeping all afternoon in her box, stretched at all the commotion, yawned, and curled back up.

J.D. squinted through the screen door, trying to see Georgie Lee. The clouds made it seem almost nighttime, and the wind sent squalls of heavy rain across the fields. Lightning crimpled in the sky all around, and the thunder was breaking so hard that it made glasses clink together in the cupboard.

"There she is!" J.D. shouted. "She's standing under one of the pine trees."

"Georgie Lee, get yourself into the barn!" Grandmother yelled.

The dark, wet form of Georgie Lee didn't move. Grandmother opened the screen door. She and J.D. waved their arms and whistled and yelled. Georgie Lee still didn't move. J.D. and Grandmother got soaked with the whipping rain.

Grandmother tried one more time. "Georgie Lee, what's wrong with you? I thought you were a smart cow!"

An enormous bolt of lightning punctured the dark clouds. As the thunder's roar died away, Grandmother and J.D. heard a puzzled moo.

The moo didn't come from the dark figure by the tree. It came from the dry safety of the barn. J.D. and Grandmother stared into the rain.

"That's not Georgie Lee," Grandmother said. "It's the hay tarp caught on the fence."

A corner of the tarp flapped in the air.

"It doesn't look anything like a cow now," J.D. said, laughing.

Grandmother started to laugh, too. "Look at us, soaking wet over a hay tarp. I guess Georgie Lee has good sense after all. That's more than I can say about us!"

Grandmother cracked a window in the bedroom, and J.D. fell asleep listening to the dripping eaves, the spicy smell of rain pulling him into sleep.

The next morning, when Grandmother gently woke J.D. for breakfast, she said, "Half of one of the big oaks is down."

J.D. ran to look.

The big oak section lay with its crown of leaves stuck ten feet into the air. In the middle of the great grounded branches, surrounded by leaves, stood Georgie Lee, sniffing curiously.

"Look, Grandmother," J.D. said.

"A cow in a tree," said Grandmother. "Now I've seen everything."

"Except hail as big as golf balls," said J.D.

5. THE HAUNTED HOUSE

J.D. found two big sticks in the old henhouse and put them in the back of the truck. Grandmother had said there might be snakes at the old Waller place, and J.D. wasn't taking any chances. When he turned around, he noticed Georgie Lee standing silently in the field.

"What's wrong with Georgie Lee?" he asked.

Grandmother shaded her eyes against the hard

sun. "Maybe she needs some fresh water."

Georgie Lee had two ponds to drink from, but they got so low and mucky in August that Grandmother always kept an old bathtub filled with fresh water from her well for the cow.

J.D. checked the tub. "It's down a little. I'll give her some more."

Georgie Lee watched J.D. drag the green hose from the pump house. When the water started to splash into the tub, she walked slowly over and took a quick drink. Then she went back and stood under the pine tree, switching her tail.

"I think she's just got the August droops," Grandmother said. "She'll be all right."

"What are August droops?" J.D. asked.

"It's what everybody and everything but me and you get in August," Grandmother said.

"Boots has it, too," J.D. said.

Grandmother's black-and-white cat walked slowly to the truck, her eyes half closed against the blazing brightness.

"Want to go with us, Boots?" J.D. asked.

Boots meowed and sat down.

"Guess not," Grandmother said.

She and J.D. climbed into the truck. The seat was so hot, J.D. had to lift his legs quickly into the air.

"Maybe we're the only ones who like August," J.D. said.

"I don't like August," Grandmother said.

J.D. let his legs drop to the seat. "But, Grandmother—"

Grandmother grinned and rolled her eyes at the ceiling. "I don't like August, I love it. And I love this coming Saturday in August most of all."

J.D. laughed.

"Nine years ago Saturday you were born at one-o-five in the morning," Grandmother said.

"And sixty-four years ago on Saturday you were born at your grandaddy's place," J.D. said.

"The best day in the whole year," Grandmother said.

"The best day ever," J.D. said.

On Saturday everybody would come to Grandmother's to celebrate the two birthdays. The house and yard would be full. But today it was just J.D. and Grandmother going to a haunted house.

"Tell me about Taz again," J.D. said as Grandmother drove down Jackson School Road.

"Taz was plowing there one day and stopped to rest under the big oak tree by the fence. He heard children running and playing back by the old house, but when he got to the house, there was nobody there. Not a sound anywhere."

"Tell John Edd's story," J.D. said.

Grandmother turned down a small gravel road. The truck thumped up and down in dry puddle holes in the road.

"John Edd was looking for one of his cows that got out. He always did have the worst luck with cows—worse than Ronald even."

J.D. stuck his arm out the window and let the hot air push it up like an airplane wing. Grandmother swerved to avoid a big hole in the road before she

continued. "That day John Edd's cows had wandered next door to have a look around. He found them, all but a big, old part-Jersey cow with one horn."

Grandmother pulled the truck over to the grass by a fence and stopped. "We're here."

All J.D. saw was a big field and a stand of trees at the back of it.

Grandmother pointed down the bumpy road they'd come on. "John Edd walked up here to the old Waller place back in those trees and heard all this thrashing around in the bushes. He thought it was his cow, but when he got closer, it got real still and quiet, and then he heard a voice say, 'We're home, come in.'"

J.D. narrowed his eyes at Grandmother. "You're

not making this up, are you?"

Grandmother narrowed her eyes at J.D. "You ought to know by now, J.D., that I don't have to make up stories. They spring up left and right around here like grass growing between your toes."

From the safety of the truck J.D. looked across the field at the tall, dark trees. Grandmother handed him one of the sticks from the back of the truck.

"We could've probably walked straight through the flat woods behind Ronald's and been here quicker, but we're going to get hot enough just walking through this field," she said.

The field was filled with crunchy, dry grass stubble where someone had cut hay.

"Did he find his cow?" J.D. asked.

"She was back in the field with the rest of them the next day," Grandmother said.

J.D. and Grandmother walked to the end of the field. Bushes and vines and tall mounds of weeds grew up to J.D.'s waist. Grandmother walked in front, waving her stick through the undergrowth before moving ahead. J.D. banged the ground behind her, hoping to scare any lurking snakes far away.

"There it is," Grandmother said.

The trees thinned out, and the old Waller place stood between two big maples. There was no yard, just more bushes and vines and weeds. The weeds next to the house had been eaten down or flattened by somebody's cows or deer or something, and there was a small worn path that led down the hill beyond the house.

The house was like two square boxes stacked on each other with a roof on top. Only one of the windows had any glass left in it, and it was a small broken bit at the bottom. A small smokehouse crumbled doorless to the side of the house.

There was no breeze or moving air at all. It was so quiet, J.D. thought he could hear the sweat drops sliding down his skin.

"Nobody's lived here for forty years," Grandmother said.

"What happened to them?" J.D. asked.

"Moved away," Grandmother said.

Grandmother and J.D. walked around the house, looking in each window. There were four rooms downstairs. The only furniture left was an old chipped painted table in what Grandmother said was the kitchen and a broken chair in the front room. Pieces of the ceiling had fallen in chunks to the floor, and water-stained wallpaper peeled and curled off the walls like leaves of a giant paper plant.

They climbed the crumbling steps to the front door.

"Careful," Grandmother said, avoiding loose and broken boards.

"It doesn't look like a haunted house," J.D. said. "It looks just like any other house around here, only older."

The door was stuck, and both J.D. and Grandmother had to push against it to shove it far enough back to allow them to squeeze inside.

It smelled like old newspapers and dust. Piles of papers fell out of boxes. Broken glass, bits of wood, and faded scraps of clothes lay on the floor. The stairs to the second floor were steep, but they looked solid.

"Can we go up?" J.D. said.

Grandmother tested the bottom two steps. "Feels solid."

Slowly Grandmother and J.D. climbed. There was one big attic room. More boxes of papers were shoved up against the stair wall. J.D. moved a piece of cardboard.

"These are really old," J.D. said, pushing at the magazines and yellowed papers with his stick. He reached to pick up a magazine, but it fell apart when he moved it.

Grandmother shifted the papers a little. Then she stopped. "What's that sound?"

J.D. held his breath. He didn't hear anything.

"Mice," Grandmother said.

J.D. and Grandmother walked around the attic, looking in more boxes.

"There's that noise again," Grandmother said.

J.D. heard it this time, too. Something was walking very softly up the attic steps. J.D. wanted to hide behind Grandmother, but he was too scared to move.

The ghost footsteps stopped. Then they came rushing up the stairs and stood before J.D. and Grandmother and meowed.

"Boots!" J.D. said, letting his breath out. "How'd you get here?"

"Followed us," Grandmother said.

Boots's little pink tongue tip stuck out in the heat. J.D. poured some water from his drink bottle into his hand. Boots licked it away with her Velcro-like tongue. Then she walked around the attic as J.D. and Grandmother had done. She stopped in a corner and pawed at something.

"What'd you find?" J.D. asked.

Grandmother pulled something long and papery from between Boots's paws.

"Snakeskin," Grandmother said. "Chicken snake. A big one."

The pale snakeskin hung from Grandmother's shoulder to the floor.

Boots began pawing at another pile of papers.

"It's another one," Grandmother said.

J.D. swallowed and pulled the second skin away from Boots. It was almost as long as the first one.

"How did snakes get upstairs?" he said.

Grandmother pointed to the sagging roof by the chimney and the hole in the chimney next to it.

"You want to look around outside for a while?" J.D. asked.

"I'm right behind you," Grandmother said.

They had to call Boots twice to get her out of the house.

J.D. rolled both snakeskins and put them in his backpack.

"We may as well check out the smokehouse," Grandmother said.

J.D. pounded at the grass with his stick.

The smokehouse was smaller than Grandmother's, and it was missing a door. Old broken jars and splintered baskets were piled on the floor. Grandmother scooted a jumble of broken crocks and jars to one side with her stick.

J.D. was bending to pick up another snakeskin

when he heard something moving in the bushes outside.

Grandmother heard it, too. She motioned J.D. to the door. There was no sign of Boots this time.

The noise became louder. When it stopped, there was no other sound anywhere, no birdsong, no fly buzzing.

The bushes started crackling again.

"Run!" Grandmother shouted.

Grandmother and J.D. leaped out of the old smokehouse and sprinted through bushes back the way they'd come in.

As soon as they were in the field, free of the dark trees and the house, J.D. and Grandmother slowed down, but whatever was chasing them was still running.

Boots stared at J.D. and Grandmother from the top of a post.

"It's coming, Boots. Run!" J.D. shouted, glancing back over his shoulder to see Georgie Lee emerge at a trot from the heavy brush.

"It's after Georgie Lee, too!" J.D. yelled to Grandmother.

Grandmother stopped running.

"Georgie Lee?" she said. Grandmother breathed hard. "Stop running, J.D. It isn't after Georgie Lee; it *is* Georgie Lee."

Georgie Lee trotted up to J.D. and Grandmother. Her sides were wet from sweat, and pieces of broken twigs and leaves stuck to her sticky hair.

"How'd Georgie Lee get here?" J.D. said.

"Pushed the fence post over again and followed Boots," Grandmother said.

"Some ghost," J.D. said, trying to sound mad.

"We can't walk Georgie Lee home down the road, so we'll have to walk back through the woods and have Taz drive us over later to get the truck," said Grandmother.

It was shady and peaceful walking along the deer path in the woods, but J.D. kept his snake stick ready just in case.

When they got back home, Boots flopped on the cool porch floor, and Georgie Lee had a long drink of water from her tub. Grandmother and J.D. had tall glasses of lemonade with ice piled to the rim of the glasses.

J.D. spread the three snakeskins on the table.

Grandmother picked up the two long ones. "Chicken snakes."

She smoothed the thin, puckered skin of the third.

"That one's different," J.D. said.

Grandmother nodded. The tail of the third skin was short and stubby. The surface had a different pattern from the first two.

"Copperhead," Grandmother said softly.

J.D. felt as if snakes were crawling

around his legs when Grandmother said that.

"There was probably a fat copperhead watching us the whole time we were there," he said.

"I've never seen but two copperheads in my life," Grandmother said. "They won't bother you if you don't bother them."

"We probably stepped on one when we were running," he said.

"Not likely," Grandmother said. "Georgie Lee stomped and thrashed around the house so loud she scared every snake off for miles."

"Good old Georgie Lee," said J.D., forgetting that if Georgie Lee hadn't scared them, they wouldn't have run so wild through the thicket in the first place.

"Well, at least Georgie Lee doesn't have the August droops anymore," J.D. added, looking in the direction of the pasture.

It was true. Georgie Lee was marching purposefully to the west field, where her favorite stand of clover grew.

As they did afternoon chores, J.D. kept thinking about the old Waller place.

"I bet it's really scary after dark," he said.

"I don't think we'll be going back to find out," Grandmother said. "Do you?"

"Nope," J.D. said, wondering if snakes slept at night.

Later in bed he was still wondering about the snakes when he heard a soft sound at the window. "Grandmother, there's something at the window," J.D. said.

Grandmother sat up in her big bed across the room. "I see it, J.D. Come over here as quietly as you can."

J.D. crept out of bed and tiptoed to Grandmother's side. "Is it a ghost?" J.D. asked.

"Shhh," Grandmother said, taking J.D.'s hand. Barefoot, she led him onto the front porch and into the moonlit yard.

On the window screen was a pale-colored moth the size of both of J.D.'s hands. Softly, silently it moved its wide wings.

"It's a luna moth," Grandmother said, "one of the grandest sights in the world."

"It looks like a ghost moth," said J.D.

"For most folks that's what they are. They hear about them but never see them," Grandmother said.

Boots appeared inside the window. She batted at the screen, trying to reach the moth. The great moth lifted away from the window and floated into the dark.

"Grandmother, maybe there's a whole colony of them deep in the woods at the Waller place," J.D. said.

"If not there, somewhere else," Grandmother said.

Back in bed J.D. heard something again at the window. He thought it was Boots, but she was curled up asleep at the foot of Grandmother's bed. The thin curtain at the side puffed out as if an invisible breeze were there.

"Grandmother, there's something else at the window," J.D. said.

"Is it another moth?" Grandmother asked.

"I don't think so. It's making puffing sounds."

"We're not the three pigs," Grandmother said, "so it can't be a wolf."

Something scraped against the screen.

"Georgie Lee, quit licking the window screen," Grandmother shouted, sitting up in bed.

"She must've heard us go outside to see the moth," J.D. said.

"Now we have to go outside again to put her up," Grandmother said.

Georgie Lee had pushed over the same fence post from the morning. Grandmother backed the truck up against the post so Georgie Lee couldn't lean on it again.

"We'll fix it for good in the morning," Grandmother grumbled.

"So she won't get out anymore," J.D. said.

"Do you think that's possible?" Grandmother asked.

J.D. watched Georgie Lee pushing at the truck bumper with her head.

"Nope," he said, smiling.

6. STARS AND DOGS

J.D. and Grandmother were clearing the attic room for the visitors for Saturday's birthday party.

"One of these days Early's going to have to get rid of some of this stuff," Grandmother said, shoving one of Early's treasure boxes into the closet.

"He can't get rid of his treasures," J.D. said.

"He could spread them out a little," said Grandmother.

J.D. liked that idea. He wondered how many boxes he could talk Mama into letting him have.

"Where's Boots?" J.D. said. There was nothing Boots liked better than jumping in and out of boxes and exploring.

"I haven't seen or heard from that cat all morning," Grandmother answered.

A long *moo* came from the field below.

"On the other hand, I've heard plenty from that cow," Grandmother said.

"Georgie Lee's shaking her head and running back and forth," J.D. said. "What's wrong with her?"

J.D. and Grandmother watched Georgie Lee.

"Maybe yellow jackets," Grandmother said at last, "or hornets or bumblebees or horseflies."

"All those?" J.D. asked.

"Not all at once," Grandmother said. "We'd better go see which it is."

Georgie Lee saw them and ran to the fence.

"I don't see any bees," J.D. said.

"No," Grandmother said. "Me either."

Georgie Lee suddenly shook her head and ran to the corner of her pasture. Then she ran back to the gate. At the same time Boots streaked across the yard and clawed up the pine tree, her ears back and her eyes wild.

"What's gotten into them?" Grandmother said.

Boots meowed. Georgie Lee mooed. Then they both ran to the corner of the field, looking toward Effie's.

"I think they're trying to tell us something," Grandmother said. "Open the gate, J.D."

"But Georgie Lee will run off," J.D. said.

"Maybe," Grandmother said.

J.D. swung the gate open.

Georgie Lee was through it and trotting toward Effie's with Boots running to keep up. Every few feet they stopped to make sure Grandmother and J.D. were following.

They weren't heading for the cornfield or Effie's house. They were going around the back through the hayfield to Effie's apple orchard on the far side of her house.

Stonewall baaed from the barn.

Boots and Georgie Lee stopped between two apple trees.

An arm raised up from the grass and waved.

"My stars!" Grandmother said.

"Is it Effie?" J.D. asked as he and Grandmother began running.

Effie smiled at them from the ground. "I knew somebody would come sooner or later," she said.

"What happened? Can you move?" Grandmother asked.

"I fell down," Effie said, "late yesterday."

"You've been lying here since then?" Grandmother almost shouted.

J.D. sank down on his knees beside Effie. "You

spent the night out here all by yourself?" he asked.

"I tried to get people's attention," Effie said. "At first I yelled, then I waved, but everybody just drove on by. Even the mailman this morning didn't see me."

"Can you get up?" Grandmother said.

"I don't know," Effie said. "It hurt so when I tried, I was afraid I'd fall again and really break something."

"J.D. can call for help," Grandmother said.

"No!" Effie said. "Here, help me. Grab my shoulders and arms, and pull me straight up."

J.D. and Grandmother slowly eased Effie to her feet. Effie moved her right foot an inch and then her left. "I can walk to the house if you help. See, nothing's broken," she said.

J.D. walked on one side of Effie, Grandmother on the other.

"That was some night," Effie said. "I watched the sun go down. I thought once or twice about crawling to the house, but I didn't. Crickets started up at dusk. It was a warm night but not much dew. Not many mosquitoes either. Too dry, I guess."

"Weren't you scared?" J.D. asked.

"Why would I be?" Effie said. "I was in my own orchard."

"Did you sleep any?" Grandmother asked.

"No," Effie said, "I was too busy."

"Busy?" J.D. said.

"I had company all night," Effie said, and laughed.

"What kind of company?" J.D. asked.

Effie laughed again.

"Every dog in the county came by to give me a sniff. Old Boomer and Taz's Maisy and the Rileys' Muffler sat by me a little while. John Edd's hound, Jasper, even howled a time or two when he came by. Every dog around knew I was lying here, but not a human soul," Effie said, shaking her head.

J.D. and Grandmother had to laugh, too, at the thought of Effie being visited by all the county dogs.

"The howling stirred up Georgie Lee," Effie said. "She started bawling, and I mooed back."

"So that's what got her going so," Grandmother said.

"My first visitor this morning was Boots," Effie said. "She stayed a long time. I thought sure somebody would see her lying on my chest purring. Finally I told her to go home and get help."

"And she did," J.D. said proudly.

"Yep," Effie said. "You and Elda and Georgie Lee."

Climbing the three steps to Effie's porch wasn't easy. Effie kept leaning backward. J.D. and Grandmother had to link their arms behind her back, as if they were playing Red Rover, to keep Effie steady.

Once in the house Effie wanted to sit in her big stuffed rocking chair. Slowly J.D. and Grandmother lowered her into it.

"Ahh, that's more like it," Effie said. "I'm wicked thirsty, J.D."

J.D. ran to get her a glass of water. Effie drank it all.

"Hungry, too?" Grandmother said.

"I was thinking of food all night," Effie said.

Grandmother headed for the kitchen.

"Iced tea'd sure be good, too," Effie called.

While Grandmother warmed up some potatoes and beans and cornbread and made iced tea, Effie motioned for J.D. to sit on the chair arm beside her.

"You know what else?" she said.

J.D. shook his head.

"I saw something last night I hadn't seen in years," Effie said. "I saw every star come out one by one. I'd forgotten how many there are. And they move. All night they move across the sky. I saw the Little Dipper and part of the Big Dipper and the evening and morning stars, too."

"You make it sound as if lying on your back in the orchard all night was an adventure," Grandmother said, bringing in Effie's lunch.

"It was wondrous. All that night around me." Effie stopped talking to chew. She took a long sip of tea.

"The dogs. The crickets. And everywhere all

around from every direction the whippoorwills calling. And all those stars." Effie leaned over to J.D. "I'm going to have to get me one of those telescopes to see the stars with."

Georgie Lee mooed from the yard. Stonewall baaed at the same time.

"He's been shut up in the barn and the hens have been in the henhouse all night," Effie said.

"I'll let them out," J.D. said.

When his door was opened, Stonewall blinked in the sun, shook his horns, and stalked off to the back of Effie's yard, where Georgie Lee was enjoying a fine patch of red clover. He stared at Georgie Lee, then joined her in the clover, too hungry to bother with a trespassing cow.

J.D. scattered feed and corn for the chickens and gave them fresh water. He and Grandmother stayed with Effie until it was almost dark.

Effie finally shooed them home, saying, "I'm going to take me a long nap and dream about stars."

Georgie Lee and Boots escorted J.D. and Grandmother home.

"They're feeling full of themselves," Grandmother said.

"They're heroes," J.D. said. "They rescued Effie."

J.D. and Grandmother finished cleaning the attic. Afterward they sat on the porch to cool off.

A soft noise made J.D. turn his head. Maisy, Taz's old speckled dog, came trotting up. She sniffed J.D. and lay down beside him.

J.D. patted Maisy's head. "Grandmother, do you think all the dogs around check on every farm each night?"

"I wouldn't put it past them," Grandmother said.

J.D. hopped off the porch. He heard the first whippoorwill of the night. Small sprays of stars began to appear in the sky.

"That would've been something to see, that parade of dogs looking in on Effie," Grandmother said from the porch. J.D. could tell from the sound of her voice that she was smiling as she said it.

"They kept her company," J.D. said.

"They watched over her," Grandmother said. "Good neighbors do that."

J.D. walked out into the yard. Georgie Lee stood in the middle of her field, her head stretched up toward the sky. "Grandmother, there's a new moon coming up, and Georgie Lee's watching it."

"Hmm," Grandmother said. "A cow that's smart and appreciates beauty, too. Now that's some cow."

"She sure is," J.D. said.

Grandmother joined J.D. They stood side by side, admiring the curve of the moon, Effie's stars, and their own smart cow while Boots circled between them, rubbing her soft face against their legs.

In the distance a dog barked. "The patrol's started," Grandmother said.

J.D. and Grandmother laughed.

Boots purred.

And Georgie Lee gave a long answering *moo*.

"Why do some people think there's
nothing to do in the country?"
J.D. asked.
"Obviously, they've never been here,"
Grandmother said.